DATE DUE

D1505292

Eric Needs Stitches

BARBARA PAVIS MARINO
photographs by Richard Rudinski

Eric Needs Stitches

▲ Addison-Wesley

Addison-Wesley Publishing Company, Inc.
Reading, Massachusetts 01867
Printed in the United States of America
    DEFGHIJK-WZ-898765432

Book designed by Charles Mikolaycak

Library of Congress Cataloging in Publication Data

Marino, Barbara Pavis, 1948–
    Eric needs stitches.

    SUMMARY: Although he is afraid, Eric goes to the
hospital emergency room to get stitches in his knee after
a bad fall.
    [1. Hospitals — Fiction. 2. Medical care — Fiction]
I. Rudinski, Richard. II. Title.
PZ7.M33878Er   [E]   78-31694
ISBN 0-201-04401-3

ACKNOWLEDGEMENT
I would like to thank Carol Anderson, R.N., who advised and supported me;
Betsy Waterman, who helped in the editing; Harold Pine and Peter Chalk,
administrators of Holyoke Hospital, Holyoke, Massachusetts, who graciously
permitted the use of the Emergency Department facilities; friends and co-
workers in that Emergency Department, who assisted and encouraged me
throughout, and the Holyoke Police Department and Forest Park Ambulance
Service, who provided the necessary personnel and equipment.
A special thanks to Susan Russo for her invaluable assistance in making my
typewritten manuscript and collection of photographs look more like a book.
Finally, thanks to my husband Ken and to David Sigelman, M.D., for their
command performances as Eric's father and Dr. Sands.

TO PARENTS AND TEACHERS

In my five years of doing emergency nursing, I have found that children who are prepared psychologically for emergency room care are usually less traumatized and more cooperative than those children who received no preparation. This story is an honest and thorough explanation of what parents and children can expect if a child needs stitches and is brought to the emergency department of a hospital.

To my son Eric and all the other children who face an emergency room experience.

Eric was in a hurry. He jumped on his bike and off he rode, pedaling faster and faster. Suddenly a large black and silver motorcycle sped by. Eric turned his head to watch. Before he knew what happened, his bicycle hit the curb. Eric landed hard on the sidewalk.

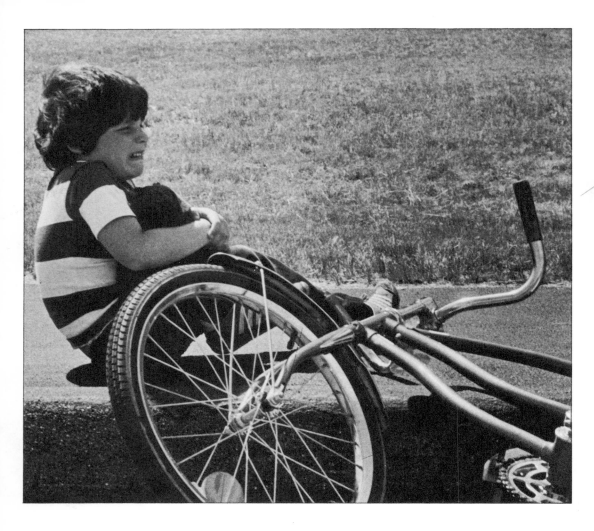

"Oooowww!" He sat up, grabbed his knee, and started to rock back and forth, crying. Through a tear in his pants he could see a large cut on his knee, which was bleeding. Suddenly he felt sick to his stomach.

Mrs. Dean, a neighbor, found him. She wrapped a piece of cloth around his knee and helped him into her car.

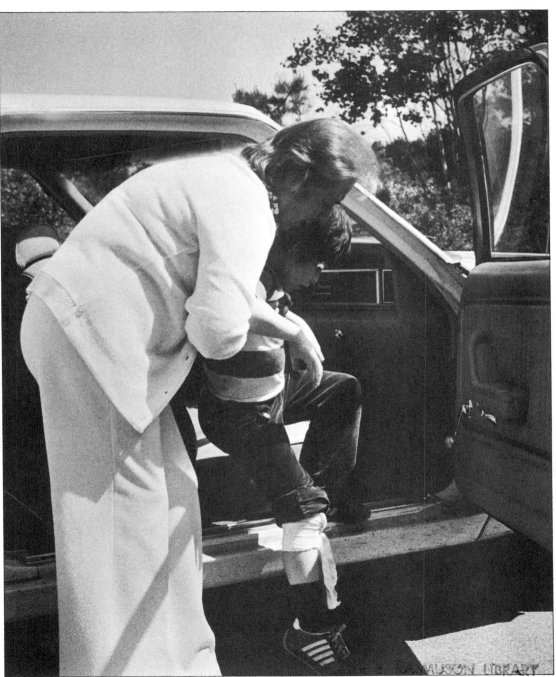

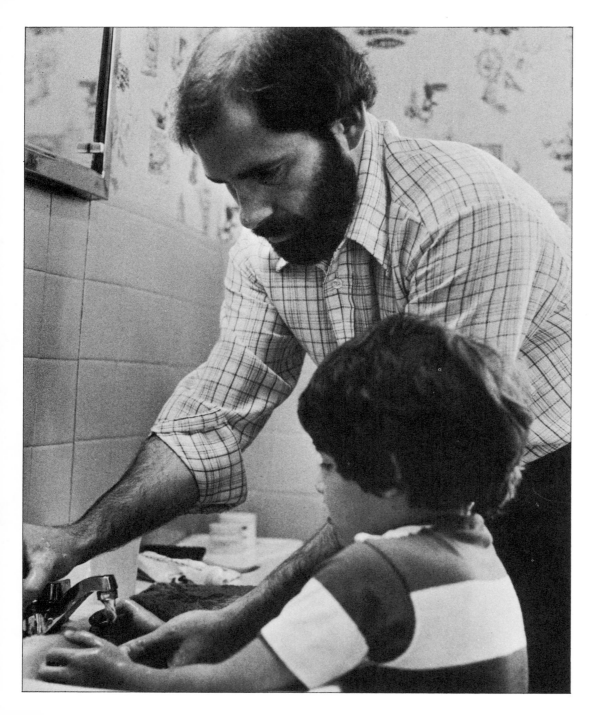

Then she drove him and his bicycle home. Eric hobbled into the house and told his father what had happened. Gently, his father washed the dirt out of the scratches on the palms of his hands. It stung and made Eric wince. Then his dad removed the cloth from the knee. Eric turned his head away. He didn't want to see it again.

His dad said that the cut was deep and wide and probably needed stitches. "Stitches!" Eric moaned. "They hurt! I don't want them!" But his father insisted that they had to go to the emergency room.

"Eric," his father explained, "there's really no choice. If we leave this cut open it could get infected. You'd have to take medicine every day, and it would hurt a lot worse than it does now. So let's leave a note for Mom and get it over with. After you're all finished we'll stop and buy a big double-scoop ice cream cone."

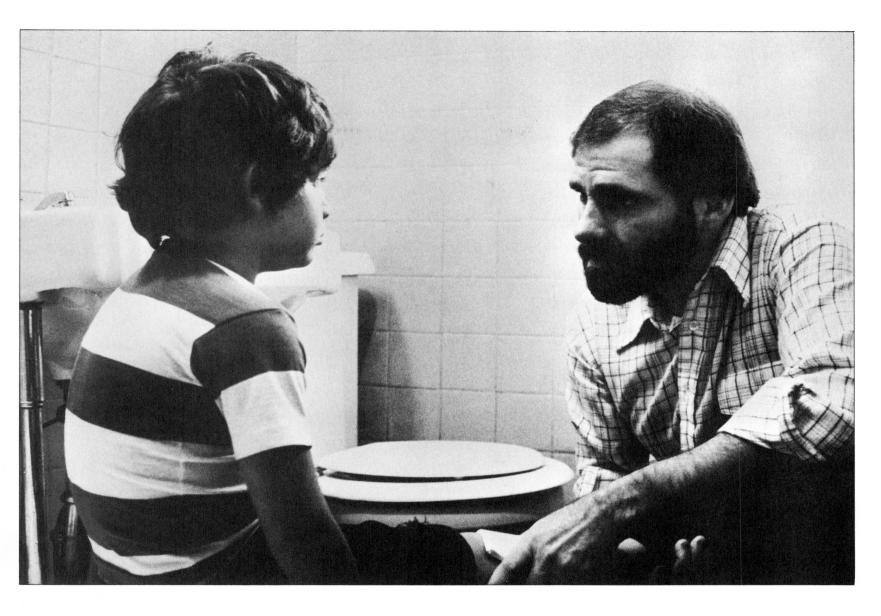

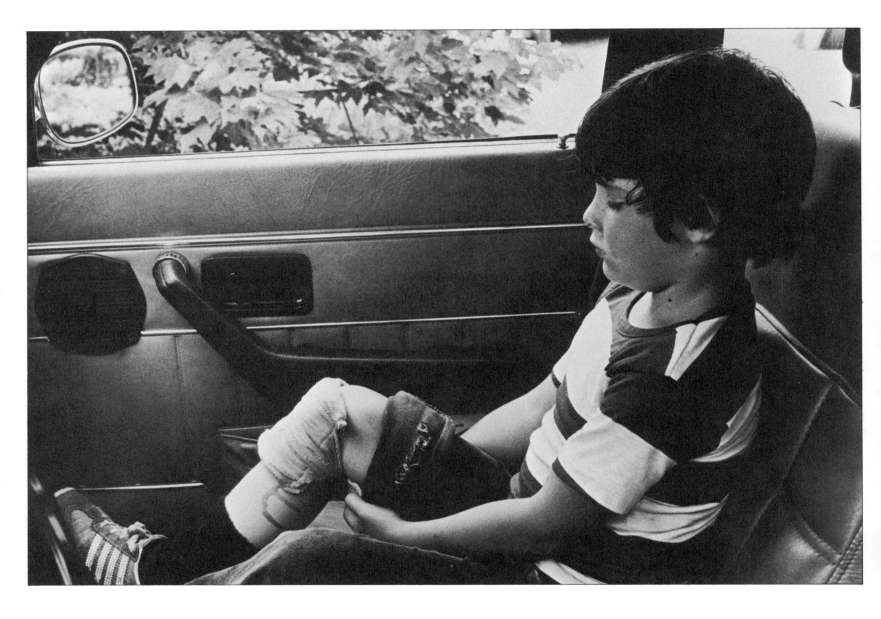

On the way to the hospital's emergency room, Eric had butterflies in his stomach. He couldn't stop talking, which is what always happened when he was afraid.

"What will they do?" he asked nervously. "Will it hurt a lot?"

"It will hurt for a minute or two," said his father. "The doctor puts some medicine into the cut with a needle; after a few minutes your knee will get numb.

"Remember the time the dentist put some medicine into your gum with a needle? After a few minutes your gum fell asleep, and you couldn't feel him drilling your tooth. Well, the doctor does almost the same thing to your knee. Then he sews the skin together with a needle and thread — the same way we fix your pants when they rip. But it won't hurt because your knee will be asleep."

"I'm really scared," Eric said. "Will you stay with me?"

"Of course I'll stay, if it's okay with the doctor. Everyone gets a little scared when something different is about to happen."

Walking toward the emergency entrance they saw an ambulance arrive. Eric stared as the attendants rolled a stretcher into the hospital. He was glad he wasn't hurt that badly.

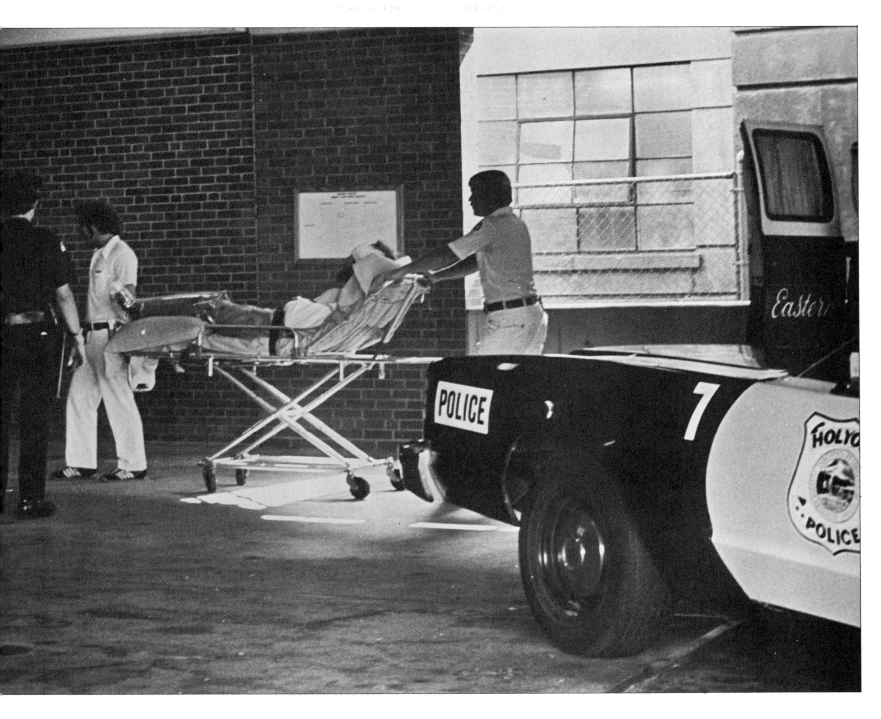

Inside the hospital, Eric's father gave some information to the receptionist behind a desk. Then they went into the waiting room. A girl sitting next to Eric had her arm in a sling and a boy across from him had his hand wrapped in a bandage. "I wonder if that kid needs stitches, too?" thought Eric.

Over a loudspeaker someone called for a doctor. Nurses rushed back and forth.

"Do we have to wait a long time?" Eric asked.

"We have to wait our turn," his father said. "People who came in ahead of us get treated first. But if you're really sick the doctor takes care of you right away, no matter whose turn it is."

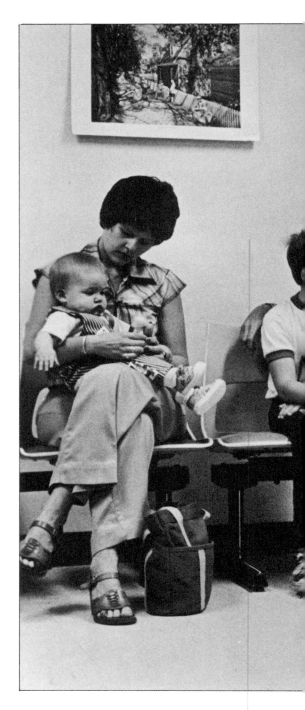

After a while a nurse came into the waiting room. "Eric Jensen," she called. Eric grabbed his dad's hand as she led them down a long hall.

The nurse told Eric that her name was Carol. She asked how he had hurt his knee.

As Eric told her about the motorcycle, they entered a strange looking room. In the center was a stretcher on wheels, with metal rails attached to either side. A big light hung above it.

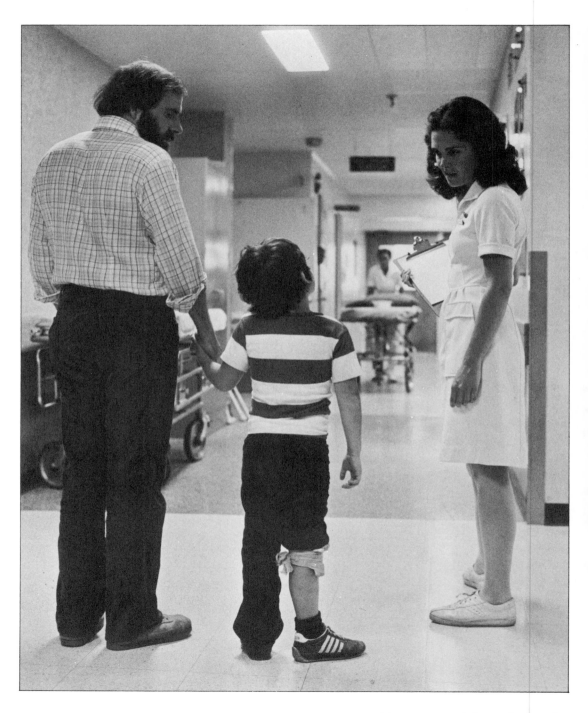

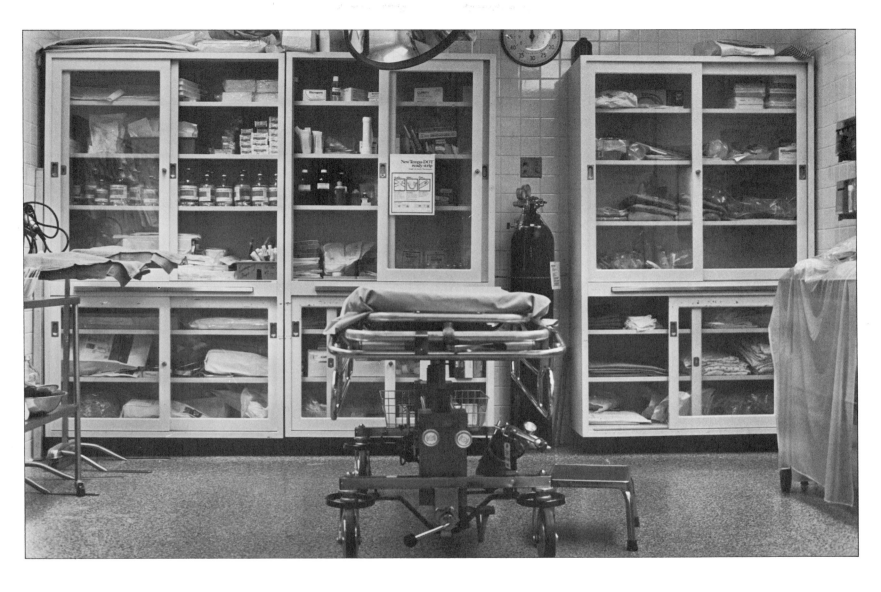

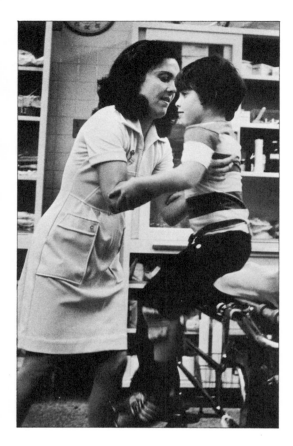

"Sit on the stretcher," she said. "I'm going to take the dressing off and see what you did to yourself." She unwrapped the bandage gently. "Well, Eric, this will need some stitches but I think we'll be able to fix you right up. What about your bike? How badly did it get hurt?" She smiled at him.

"It looked okay. I think I only scratched up the fender." Eric grinned back at her, beginning to feel better.

"Have you ever had stitches before?" the nurse asked.

"No, but my dad explained it to me. Can he stay with me?"

"If it's okay with the doctor," she replied. "And you have a very important job to do. You have to try very hard not to move your leg. Do you think you can keep it still?"

"I'll try, but I'm afraid. What if I cry?"

"If you're scared and it hurts, go ahead and cry. The most important thing is to keep your leg still so the doctor can fix it."

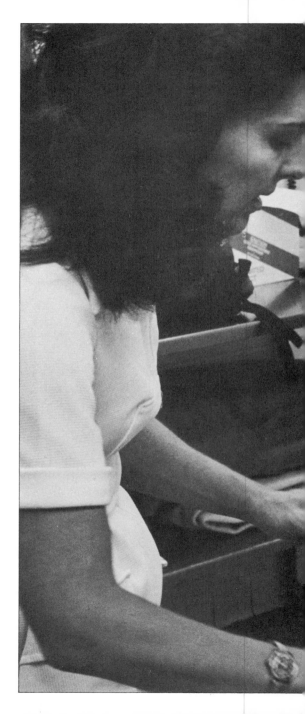

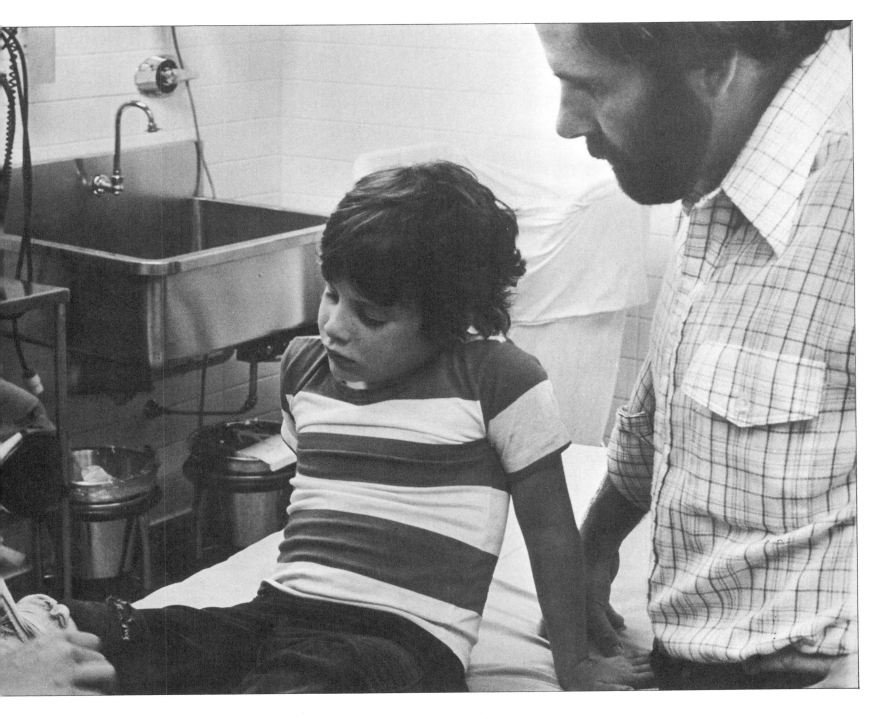

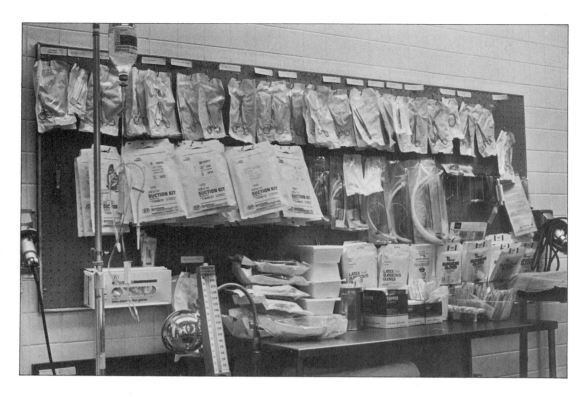

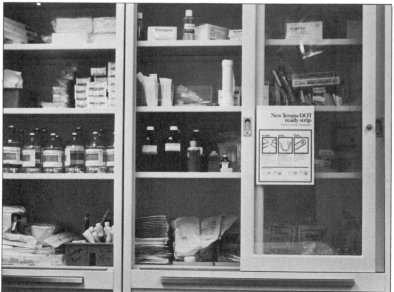

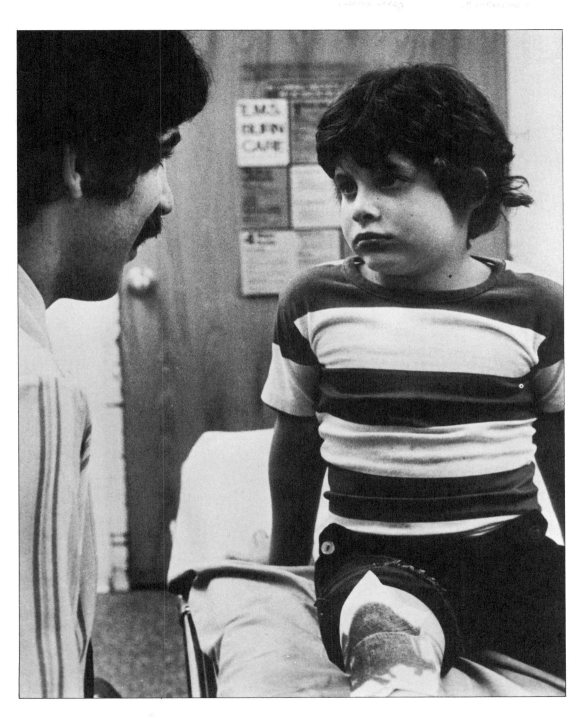

After the nurse left, Eric looked around the room. Against the walls were all sorts of things: bandages, shiny metal tools, medicine bottles, and many other things he'd never seen before. From the ceiling hung the large light, which could be moved from one end of the stretcher to the other.

Before long the nurse returned with the doctor.

"Eric, this is Dr. Sands," she said.

"Hello, Eric," the doctor said, smiling. "I hear you fell off your bike and cut your knee. You've never had stitches, right?"

"Right," Eric answered, his voice trembling. He wanted to jump off the stretcher and run away.

"Okay, then we'll tell you everything we're going to do. Your father can stay as long as you do what we ask," the doctor said, motioning to Eric's father to stand next to the head of the stretcher.

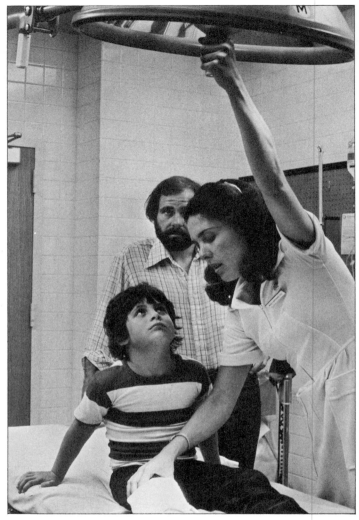

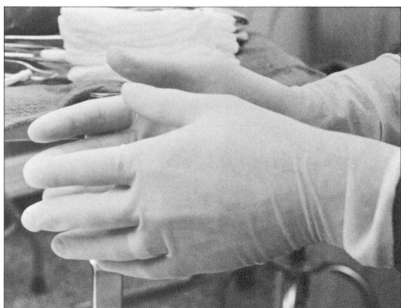

As the nurse pulled up a small table she said, "These tools are called instruments and the doctor uses them when he sews the cut together." On the stand were towels, scissors, tweezers, bandages, a metal dish filled with a brown, soapy liquid, and a syringe with two needles next to it. The doctor put on rubber gloves while the nurse turned on the big light and swung it around so it shone directly on the cut. Then Dr. Sands placed a green towel with a hole in its center right over Eric's knee.

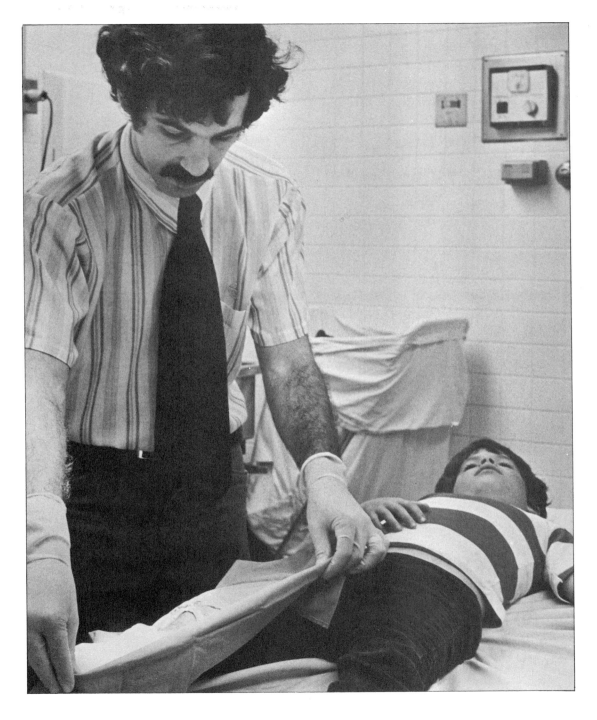

"Eric," said the doctor, "I'm going to use this needle to put some medicine into the cut. Your knee will sting for a minute and then get numb."

"I'm scared," Eric said, trying not to cry.

"We know you're scared," the nurse said. "Look at your father and squeeze his hand really tight when it hurts."

"It's very important that you don't move your leg," the doctor told him. He started to put the medicine into Eric's knee.

Eric grabbed his father's hand. "Ooww! That hurts!" he yelled, squeezing his dad's hand tighter and tighter. He tried very hard not to move, but his leg got stiff and he couldn't stop it from shaking a little.

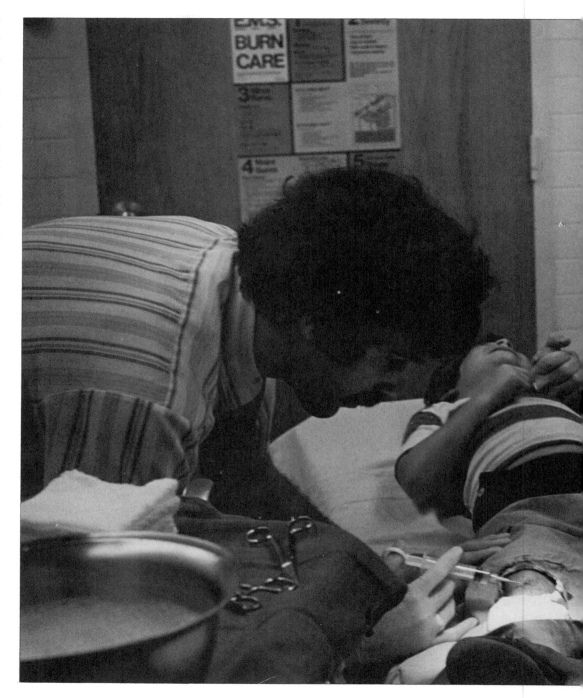

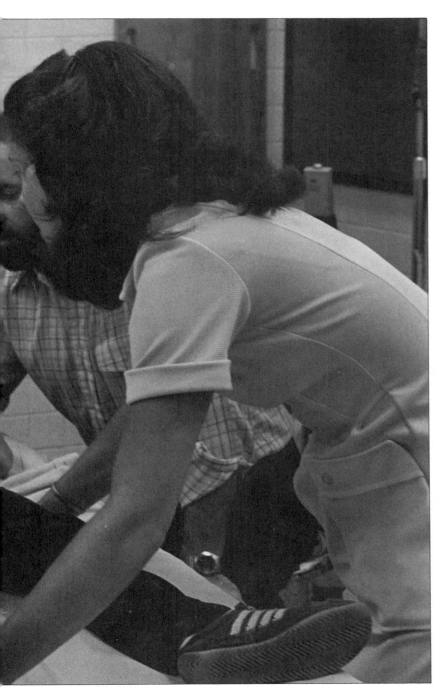

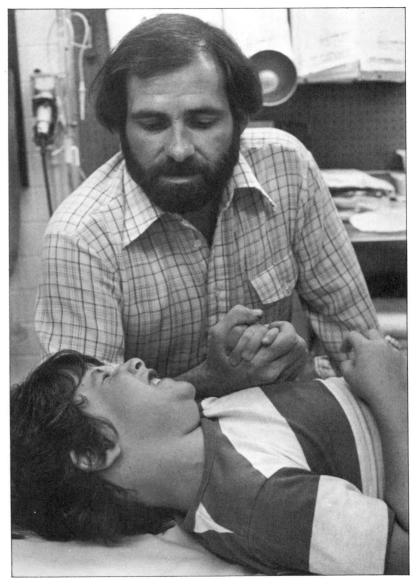

27

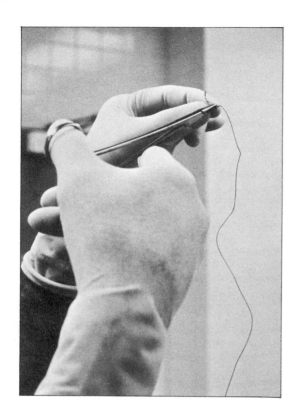

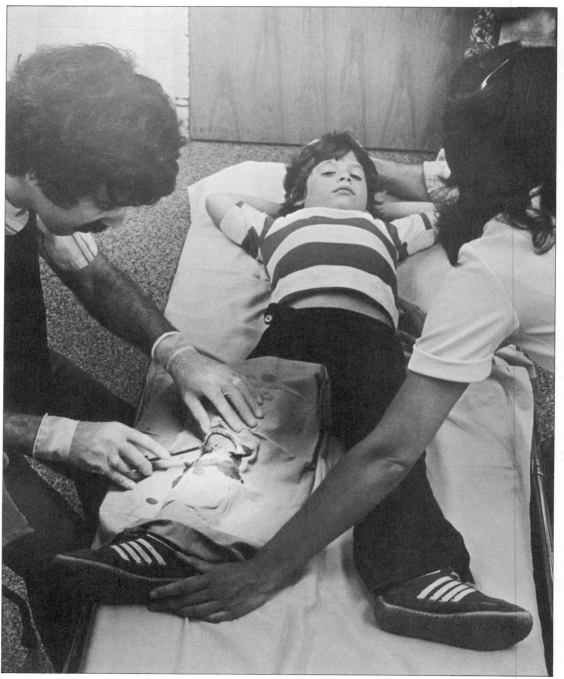

"Okay, we're finished with this part," said the doctor. "In a minute or two your knee will be numb. You did a good job keeping your leg still."

"That wasn't too bad. But I'm glad it's all over," Eric said with relief.

"Now we're going to scrub it and then sew it up with a small needle and thread. You'll be able to feel me touching your knee but it won't hurt."

Eric felt some pressure while the doctor washed his knee with the brown solution in the basin. "Dad, it doesn't hurt one bit!"

"I'm glad, Eric. I guess the worst part is over." He smiled back at Eric.

Again, Eric felt only a little bit of pressure as the doctor sewed the skin together. When he was finished, the doctor looked up at Eric's father. "These stitches can be taken out by your own doctor in about a week."

Then he shook Eric's hand. "Good job," he said. "You should be proud of yourself."

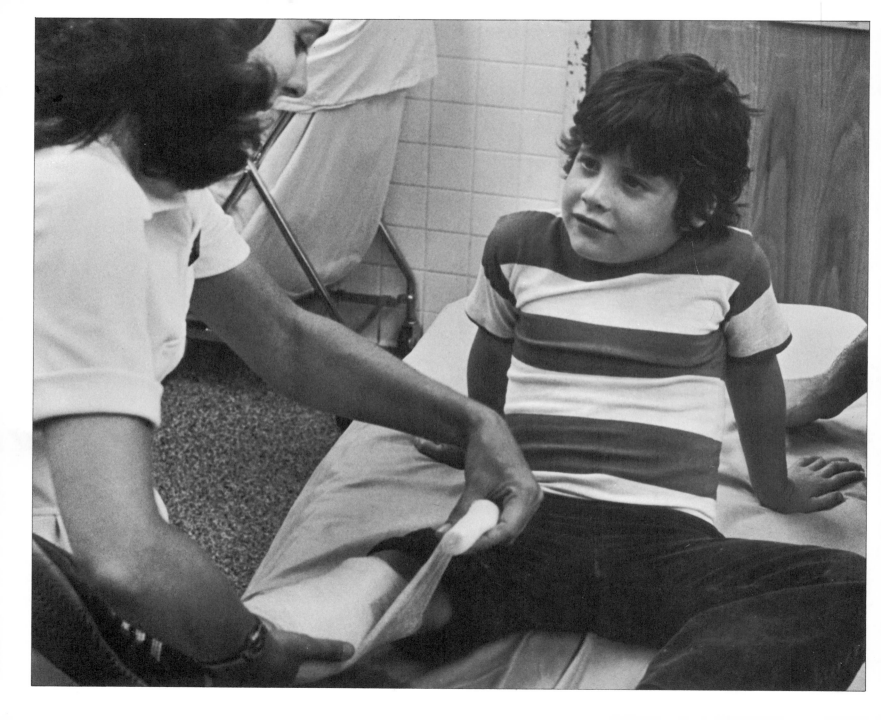

The nurse wrapped Eric's knee in a bulky, white dressing.

"Now you have another very important job to do," she said. "This bandage has to stay clean and dry for one week. It's your responsibility; your mom and dad can't be with you all the time to remind you. If this dressing gets wet or dirty you could still get an infection, even with the stitches. Do you think you're big enough to take care of it?"

Eric nodded. "I'll try," he said.

Carol helped him off the stretcher. "You were very good," she said. "Dr. Sands is right, Eric. You should be proud."

His father grinned and put his arm around Eric. "Do you think he deserves a double-scoop ice cream cone?" he asked.

"I sure do," the nurse replied as she opened the door.

Eric grinned back at them both. "Let's go," he said. And that's just what they did.

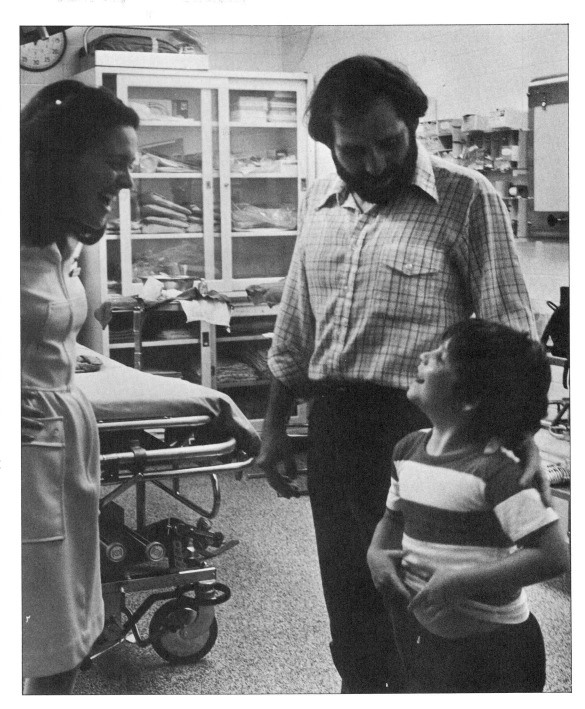

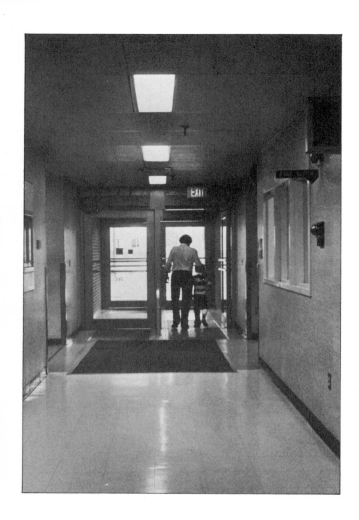